Text copyright © 2012 by the Estate of Russell Hoban
Illustrations copyright © 2012 by Quentin Blake

First U.S. edition 2012

Library of Congress Cataloging-in-Publication Data is available.

Library of Congress Catalog Card Number pending

ISBN 978-0-7636-6400-8

12 13 14 15 16 17 scp 10 9 8 7 6 5 4 3 2 1

Printed in Humen, Dongguan, China

This book was typeset in Adobe Garamond.
The illustrations were done in pen and watercolor.

Candlewick Press
99 Dover Street
Somerville, Massachusetts 02144

visit us at www.candlewick.com

Russell Hoban & Quentin Blake

Rosie's Magic Horse

CANDLEWICK PRESS

There was an ice-pop stick with
ice-cold sweetness all around it, white
on the inside, pink on the outside.

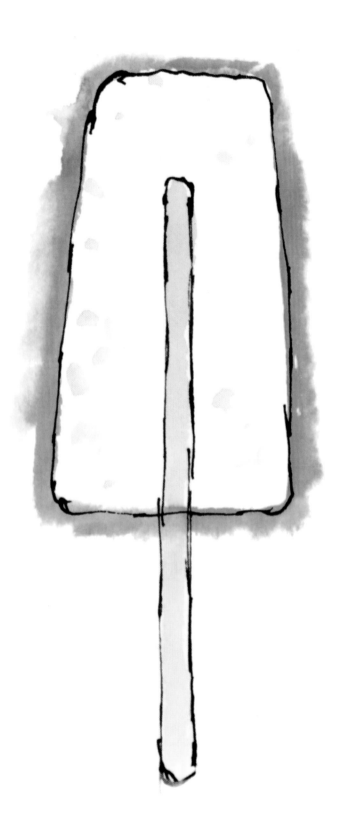

Then the sweetness was gone, and the stick
fell to the ground. "The sweetness is gone,"
said the stick. "No more sweetness."

For a long time, nothing happened.

There was wind, there was rain,

there were brown leaves blowing.

Then a hand picked up the ice-pop stick.

The hand belonged to a girl named Rosie.

She put the stick in her cigar box

with her other ice-pop sticks.

"Without our ice-pops, we are nothing,"

said the oldest stick.

"I am not nothing," said the new stick.

"I could be something."

"What?" said the old stick.

"Maybe a horse," said the new stick.

"In your dreams," said the old stick.

"We'd like to be a horse, too,"

said some of the other sticks.

That night they dreamed of being a horse.

The next night, when Rosie went to say good night to
her mom and dad, they were sitting at the kitchen table,
shaking their heads over a big pile of bills. "I don't know
how we're going to pay these," said her dad.

Before Rosie went to sleep, she said, "I wish my cigar box was a chest full of treasure to pay bills with."

She was fooling around with the ice-pop sticks when she saw that her hands had made an ice-pop-stick horse.

"A horse can't pay the bills," said Rosie, and she fell asleep.

When the clock struck midnight, the horse galloped out of the cigar box.

Rosie woke up just in time to jump on its back.

"My name is Stickerino," said the horse. "Where to?"

"Anywhere there's treasure," said Rosie.

"No problem," said Stickerino.

They galloped over

cities and jungles. . . .

They galloped over oceans and deserts . . .

until they came to an ice-pop mountain.

"There it is," said Stickerino. "Ice-cold treasure, sweet and frozen."

"Wrong treasure," said Rosie. "I want the kind that pirates bury in a chest."

"Can do," said Stickerino. They galloped to the other side of the mountain, and there was a sandy beach and some pirates with large and small chests full of treasure.

"That's a pretty tough crowd," said Rosie. "How am I going to get some of that gold?"

"Leave it to me," said Stickerino.

He disguised himself as an ice-cream cart and jingled his ice-cream tune.

All the pirates came running and lined up for ice cream while Rosie grabbed the biggest treasure chest she could carry and ran.

One of the pirates saw her. "Stop, thief!" he shouted, and all of the pirates started running after Rosie.

Quickly, Stickerino uncarted himself and became a swarm of flying ice-pop sticks.

When they hit the pirates, they stickled them and kept stickling them until the pirates fell down, laughing helplessly.

Stickerino rehorsed himself,
Rosie jumped on his back with
her gold, and off they went!

They galloped over deserts and oceans,
jungles and cities, until they got home.

The next morning, when Rosie's dad came down to
breakfast, he saw the chest of gold on the table.
"Where did this come from?" he asked.

"It was a long gallop,"
Rosie said, and kissed
him good morning.

"It certainly was," said all the sticks.

And they went back to sleep.

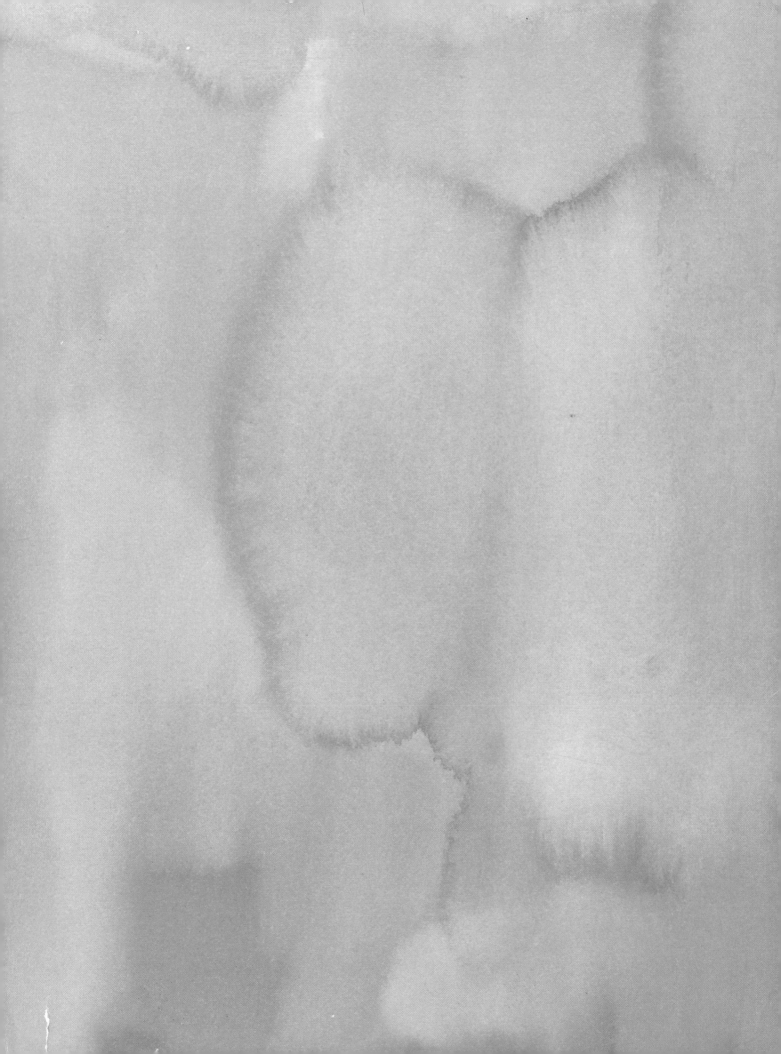